Dear Parents,

As the creator of **Go! Go! Sports Girls** and the founder of **Dream Big Toy Company**, I would like to thank you for giving your child the gifts of reading and healthy life-skills.

Healthy habits start early. I created **Go! Go! Sports Girls** as a fun and educational way to promote self-appreciation and the benefits of daily exercise, smart eating and sleeping habits, self-esteem, and overall healthy life-skills for girls. Author Kara Douglass Thom and illustrator Pamela Seatter have taken this dream a step further by creating a series of fun and educational books to accompany the dolls. Now your child can **Read & Play**.

The books have been written for the child who has begun to read alone, and younger children will enjoy having the stories read to them.

I believe every child should have the opportunity to **Dream Big and Go For It!**

Sincerely,

Jodi Bondi Norgaard

Jodi Bondi Norgaard

For our very own sports girls Grace, McKenna, Kendall, Jocie Claire, Kaelie, Maia, and Michaela, and their brothers Peter, Ben, Blake, and Alex, who inspire us every day...and for Scout, Darby, Zoe, Dixie, Ginger, and Pepper, our furry friends.
— JBN, KDT, PS, SRB

First published in 2014

Series Editor: Susan Rich Brooke

Text © 2014 by Kara Douglass Thom

Illustrations © 2014 by Pamela Seatter

Jodi Norgaard, Founder and C.E.O.
Dream Big Toy Company™
PO Box 2941, Glen Ellyn, IL 60138

www.gogosportsgirls.com

Library of Congress Control Number: 2013951459

First Edition

8 7 6 5 4 3 2 1

This book was printed in 2014 at Starprint Vietnam Co., Ltd. in 104/4-1, 2-4 Road, Amata Industrial Zone, Long Binh Ward, Bien Hoa City, Dong Nai Province, Vietnam.

ISBN 978-1-940731-04-9

Runner Girl Ella's Story

Family Fun Run

Dream Big Run Fast!

Written by Kara Douglass Thom

Illustrated by Pamela Seatter

Dream Big Toy Company™

Ella became a runner because she *needed* to.

Well, what she really *needed* was a *dog*. Ella was sure of that. But whenever she asked her parents, they told her they weren't sure she could take care of a dog.

"Maybe when you're older, Ella," her mom or dad would say. "I don't know if you're responsible enough yet." Then Ella would tell her parents that she *was* responsible. It never worked.

The Need for Speed

Even the earliest humans needed to run. They ran to hunt animals for food and clothing, and they ran to get away from danger.

Around 776 BCE, the first Olympic Games were held in Greece. At first, there were only five events. Three of them were running races.

Women didn't compete in Olympic track-and-field events until 1928. In 1984, Joan Benoit Samuelson won the first women's Olympic marathon.

One day, she decided to *show* them. She marched across the street to Mr. Peterman's house and asked if she could take his dog, Sparky, for a walk. Mr. Peterman was happy to hand over the leash.

"Hold on tight!" he said.

And that's how Ella started running.

Sparky ran down the street with Ella hanging on to the leash behind him. They ran fast and hard to the park. When Sparky stopped to sniff under a honeysuckle bush, Ella caught her breath. Then Sparky tugged the leash, and they ran on the path through the park.

Ella smiled as she breathed in the warm spring air. When she first started running, her legs felt heavy. But after a few minutes, she felt light, like a hummingbird, ready to rise up and fly.

Running Rhythms

A "tempo" is a run that includes an easy warm up and easy cool down, with a fast pace in the middle.

Runners usually run less in the week before a big race to rest their muscles. This is called "tapering."

Pick Up the Pace!

Your "pace" is how fast you run. The best running time you've ever had is called a "Personal Record," or PR for short.

When Ella brought Sparky back home,
Mr. Peterman handed her a few dollars.
"Thank you, Mr. Peterman!" Ella said.
Now she was learning how to take care of a dog
and earning money to pay for her own dog.

"Could you come back tomorrow?"
Mr. Peterman called after her as she turned to
leave. "Sparky would really enjoy another run."

Ella ran with Sparky every day after school. She also ran with Otis, Mrs. Kraft's dog, on Wednesday afternoons. And she ran with Daisy, the Vogels' dog, on Saturday mornings.

Ella discovered that she loved running as much as she loved her new dog friends. She liked to feel her heart beating inside her chest. In the morning, she could feel her leg muscles as she got out of bed. Before, she hadn't really noticed these body parts.

Running made Ella aware that there was a whole body attached to her head. Even her head felt better after running. Homework didn't seem as hard to do at night as it used to be.

Get in Gear!

Here are some things you'll need for running:

- Sneakers and socks
- Athletic shorts and shirt
- Hat or visor
- Sunscreen
- Water bottle

There was only one problem. As Ella ran with more and more neighborhood dogs, she started to run out of time.

"Hey Jon," she said to her brother. He was sitting on the couch playing a video game, and muttering something about "points" and "levels."

"Jon!" she said louder, moving closer and waving in front of the screen.

"Hold on!" he shouted without looking up.

Ella knew Jon wanted to buy a new video game. She stood right in front of him and said, "I have ten dollars to give you—do you want it or not?"

Jon finally looked up at her.

"Do you?" Ella repeated.

"Yeah!"

"Okay, get off the couch and come with me."

"Where are we going?" Jon asked. "Where's my ten bucks?"

"There will be three dollars coming from the Herricks and another three dollars from Mrs. Roy and four dollars from the Franklins...after you run with their dogs."

"Awww, Ella!" cried Jon. But he didn't turn back. Ten dollars was too tempting.

Jon and Ella ran with their dog clients three days a week. Jon didn't love running the same way that Ella did, but he really wanted to get that new game.

Ella was sure Jon would stop helping after he saved up enough money, but he didn't. He kept running with her and the dogs. And they picked up even more clients on the weekend.

The dog business was booming. Ella and Jon had more dogs than they could handle. They went to talk to their mom about it one afternoon, while she checked e-mail at the kitchen table.

"Mom, we could use another dog runner tonight," Ella said. "The Martins asked if we could get Harvey out for a run."

"How about asking one of your pals?" her mom asked, without taking her eyes off the screen.

"How about *you*, Mom?" Jon asked.

"Me?" Mom looked up from her computer. "I'd really like to, but...but I've got so much to do."

"Just twenty minutes, Mom," Ella said. "Come with us, please?"

Go Fast, Go Slow!

When a runner speeds up
for a certain distance or amount of time,
and then slows down for a certain distance
or amount of time, this is called an "interval."

"Fartlek" is a Swedish word that
means "speed play." Look for an object,
like a tree or a mailbox, and speed up
until you reach it. Then slow down until
you feel like sprinting again.

From then on, their mom ran with Harvey, the Martins' dog, on Monday nights.

And on Thursday nights, their dad managed Cootie, who belonged to Mr. Mendez. Cootie sometimes ran too fast for Ella to keep up. She was happy to turn over the leash to her dad. And her dad, who had been complaining lately that his pants didn't fit the way they used to, was happy to get the exercise.

One Sunday morning over banana pancakes, Ella's mom said, "I was thinking...since we've all been running, maybe we should enter the Pine Valley 5K Race? The race is going to help the local dog shelter. It might close down if they don't raise enough money by the end of summer."

Ella thought that was a great idea. She and Jon handed out race flyers to their neighbors and classmates.

Their dad measured a 3.1-mile route in the neighborhood so they could train. The whole family ran the practice route together. They all had to get used to running without dogs to tug them along.

What's the Distance?

Some races are short sprints, some are long runs, and some are in between!

- Track-and-field races are on an indoor or outdoor track. A track is an oval surface with different lanes for runners. Once around an official track is 400 meters (about a quarter of a mile). Track events include sprints that are one lap or shorter, all the way up to long-distance races of 25 laps! Your school or community might have a track-and-field team.

- Cross-country races are outside. The most common distance is a 5K (five kilometers or 3.1 miles). Cross country is both an individual and a team sport. Runners are judged on individual times, and they also earn points for their team.

- Road races take place on town or city streets. The most popular is a 5K. Other distances are 10K (10 kilometers or 6.2 miles), half-marathon (13.1 miles), and marathon (26.2 miles).

Finally, it was race day!

Friends and neighbors gathered with Ella and her family at the starting line. Then the gun went off—**pop!**—and Ella moved with the mass of people down the road.

When the pack loosened up, Ella zigged and zagged her way around the slower racers. As soon as she had some space, she looked for Jon and her parents. But she couldn't see them anywhere in the crowd.

Ella started to worry. Should she slow down? Should she turn around and find her family?

Road Race Rules

Get ready... Wear your race number, and your timing chip too, if the race provides one.

Get set... The fastest runners start in front, and the slowest start in the back. Try to start in a place where you will run about the same pace as other runners.

Go! Find out the race course before you start, and follow the marked course as you run.

"Go on, Ella!" she heard her mom shout from behind. "Keep running! You've got this! We'll see you at the finish line."

It was good to hear her mom's voice. Ella set her gaze on the course ahead, pumped her arms, and ran.

At the first mile marker, Ella noticed Mr. Mendez waving at her from the side of the road. Beside him was Cootie, with his long legs and huge paws. Ella buzzed along, trying to run as fast as Cootie always did.

At the halfway point, she grabbed a cup of water and saw Mr. Peterman and Sparky. Sparky barked as if to say, "Way to go, Ella!" She leaned into her run and imagined Sparky pulling her ahead on his leash.

When Ella passed the banner for mile three, she knew the race would be over soon. There were more people on the side of the road. The cheering was louder, and the barking was too.

Even though her body felt like slowing down, Ella picked up her pace...

...and sprinted across the finish line.
Ella felt fantastic!

She jogged over to pet Daisy and Otis, who were wagging their tails and woofing their congratulations. Even though Ella still didn't have a dog of her own, she had made a lot of special furry friends.

The volunteers took the tag off Ella's race number and put a shiny gold finisher's medal around her neck. Then she turned around to cheer for Jon, her mom, and her dad, who were getting close to the finish chute.

"Go Mom! Go Dad! Go Jon!" Ella shouted.

Ella and her family hugged and
high-fived each other for running the whole
race. Then, happy and hungry, they walked
over to a tent to get water and healthy snacks.

As she peeled her banana, Ella noticed the tent next to them. The Pine Valley Dog Shelter had dogs ready for adoption.

"Why don't we go take a look?" her dad said.

"Have you seen this one?" asked a volunteer. "Only ten months old, and she's house-trained already. We don't know what breed she is."

Ella knelt down to pet the puppy's sleek black ears. Her tail wagged wildly. Her eyes, round and longing, met Ella's gaze.

Ella looked at her parents, who nodded and smiled. Then she looked at the pup again.

"Oh, and she really loves to run," the volunteer added.

"We'll take her!" Ella said.

Here's What Ella Learned:

- Be creative and don't give up when you are working toward a goal.

- Build a team to help you succeed.

- Exercise is good for your body and your mind. It helps you grow healthy and strong, and also improves your focus.

- Sometimes what you hope for turns out even better than you expected.

Runner Girl Ella's Healthy Tips:

- **Warm up**. Start your runs by walking or running slowly.

- **Eat up**. Natural snacks like raisins or carrots give you more energy than sugary snacks.

- **Drink up**. To replace the water you lose when you sweat, drink water, rather than sodas or sugary drinks.

- **Layer up**. Wear layers of clothing that you can take off or put on easily as you warm up or cool down.

- **Cover up**. Always put on sunscreen to protect your skin when you run outside.

- **Rest up**. Get lots of sleep every night, especially before a big race.

Dream Big and Go For It!